This special signed
edition is limited to
1000 numbered copies.

This is copy __596__ .

James Patrick Kelly

KING OF THE
DOGS,
QUEEN OF THE
CATS

JAMES PATRICK KELLY

Subterranean Press 2020

First Edition

ISBN
978-1-59606-934-3

Subterranean Press
PO Box 190106
Burton, MI 48519

subterraneanpress.com

Manufactured in the United States of America

*For the members of
the Cambridge Science Fiction Writers Workshop.
Thanks for twenty-five years of close reading.
You made a difference.*

SCOFFLAW

Gio decided to spend the rest of his morning looking for the mystery circus. Then the paintbomb went off.

It wasn't so much an explosion as a sharp crack, like a heavy bough snapping in a windstorm. Gio jumped in alarm, staggered and had to catch himself on one of the plaza's benches. The explosive had been left in a trash can beneath the statue of Leeol Gamane. Another smart bomb imported from who-knew-where in space, fortunately programmed for upshot rather than scattershot. Gio realized he was clenching his jaw so hard that his teeth ached. He whistled to remind himself he was all right. Nobody was trying to kill anybody. Yet.

Gio had never witnessed an attack firsthand before. The front half of the statue was splattered with red paint and a plume of ruddy smoke boiled into the sky, announcing the latest casualty in what his clone Fra was calling the War Against Architecture. He glanced around to see who else had witnessed the explosion. He was the only human in this corner of the plaza. A couple of cats in suits, government clerks probably, peeked from behind the base of another statue. He called to them to see if they were all right but they skittered away as if he were the bomber. And here already were the maintenance dogs, a cur on hind legs pushing a wobbly utility cart, and a mastiff trotting alongside on all fours. They parked in front of the mess and the cur lifted solvent and a bucket from the cart while the mastiff tore off its heavy walking mitts and pulled on flexible rubber gloves. Gio's earstone buzzed with an alert from the official Supremacy feed warning of imminent attack and he decided to check in at home.

Messaging 1/34/498 Time 0927

Gio: Don't worry, I'm fine. Feeds have it wrong as usual. Just a paintbomb. Saw it go off but it was programmed for propaganda, like all the others. Nobody hurt, no ravening hordes of dogs and cats marching to overthrow the government. Just a couple of bureaucrats spooked by an exploding trash bin. Splattered the statue of old Leeol, but she's been dead—what—a hundred years? Book history. Nobody cares anymore, not even her clones.

Fra: Relieved to hear you're all right but why were you wandering around the plaza? You were supposed to be at the consensus this morning vetting the new import fees.

Gio: Showed up at the Senate, but no quorum, so consensus adjourned until tomorrow. Did my due diligence, so your turn now.

Hali: Excuse me, but the point of paintbombing another statue?

Gio: Shows how the Supremacy is losing control of the city despite the crackdown?

Hali: What crackdown?

Fra: Skip the politics and just get back here. You can take my place on the 1230 tour. I need to denounce this latest atrocity on the Senate floor.

End Session 1/34/498 Time 0936

Gio cut the feed without bothering to reply. Atrocity? More like vandalism. A prank. Fra thought he could order him around just because he was Gio's grandclone. It wasn't fair; the 1230 was Fra's tour. Gio wasn't just an extra Barbaro; he was an individual with his own plans. Nothing like his ambitious grand, despite the curse of their identical chromosomes. Fra believed he was destined to restore the failing Villa Barbaro and rule the Supremacy as their long line of grandclones once had. Gio knew better. And so did their wife, Hali.

He was just blocks from home, but he was now determined to spite bossy old Fra, so he slipped off his senatorial sash and pocketed it. The two Barbaros shared their house's seat in the mostly useless Senate. No sense in advertising his status if he was going to search for the circus. He checked to see if anyone had noticed him but the maintenance dogs were on their hind legs, getting busy with mops. Then he clipped his lawnball scarf around his neck and left the plaza, losing himself in the nervous crowd of tourists and bureaucrats and caretakers. They'd gone to ground on first report of an explosion but now were streaming back to Longview Parade, with its consensus galleries and law palaces and history arcades and gleaming monuments to the dead grands of the Enlightened City. Gio jogged up the stairs of the Academy of the Thousand Worlds, slipped through the lobby and out the other side. He waited a moment to see if anyone was following him. Satisfied that he was on his own, he strolled west on the Spaceway.

The grand boulevard was eight lanes wide here in Capital Ward and was flanked by stern blocks of government offices where clerks counted taxes and engineers planned sewers and police sorted out troublemakers. Street traffic was light after the morning rush; commuter busses had largely given way to delivery trucks. There was some sparse human foot traffic but dogs and cats filled their separate lanes on the sidewalk as they went about the day's chores. An unruly group of school pups, probably on a class trip to tour one of the Grand Houses, maybe even Villa Barbaro, was spilling out of its lane. A harried teacher whistled for order even as one pup nosed along the pavement toward a trio of adult cats in clerks' vests. A bored hiss sent the straggler scurrying back to its class.

Hard up against the city wall in Oldgate Ward was the sprawl of the Central Pound. In the late morning, most maintenance crews were out and about, but in an open bay Gio spotted a pack of firedogs washing a yellow ladder truck. They recognized him and yipped a greeting. Gio pressed a finger to his lips and nodded over his shoulder in the direction of the Grand Houses of Capital Ward. They barked in acknowledgement; they would keep his secret. While many senators had cat leanings, Gio was well known as a friend to dogs.

Messaging 1/34/498 Time 1015

Hali: Don't do this to me, Gio. I can't stand it when he sulks. Where are you? Come rescue me.

Fra: Cut off. Is that him, Hali? Cut right now! Gio, you'd better be on your way.

End Session 1/34/498 Time 1016

Gio sighed. He might've tried to explain himself to Hali if Fra hadn't butted in. Fra aspired to rule, if not the Supremacy, then at least his family. Too bad he had no talent for command. Gio sympathized with Hali, but she'd chosen Fra after all. Gio had been just a boy when they married, and even years later, he still did not quite understand their relationship. Hali was an upsider, born on a planet called Franks, who had immigrated to Boon under shadowy circumstances. Maybe she had taken up with Fra because she believed he might realize his lofty ambitions. Maybe Fra had married this exotic woman because her understanding of the Thousand Worlds

KING OF THE DOGS, QUEEN OF THE CATS

might help him politically. But Fra had been everywhere frustrated and the native grands had never accepted Hali. In any event, now that he was an adult, Gio was married to Hali as well. They had even become occasional lovers, although more out of duty than passion. She was still more Fra's wife than his, although recently she'd been acting like she regretted being married to either of the Barbaro clones. As ever, Gio thought it best to leave it to them to sort their troubles out.

The shops and restaurants of Oldgate Ward catered to the canine trade, although a handful of tourists, both human and uplifted cats, poked around the outdoor stalls and sunned themselves at the cafés. Fra thought it unseemly for a senator to mingle with this crowd, but Gio preferred the company of common citizens, no matter what species. He was tempted to set up at an outdoor table with a cup of soupy kahve or a flute of snooker and chat with passersby. But no, he needed to focus. This morning was about the circus.

Officially the Enlightened City extended only to the wall that Gio's great-great-great grandclone Pao Barbaro had built two hundred years before, but everyone regarded the outer wards that spilled from its eleven gates as part of it as well. The largest of these was Puppytown, accessed from Oldgate, Blackdoor and the Arch of the Sky. While the Spaceway on this side of the wall continued its broad progress toward the upsiders' new spaceport, the buildings on either side of it were no longer built of stone or gleaming synthetics. Narrow windows squinted through humble brick or block or tilt-up concrete facades, all painted in the narrow spectrum of colors visible to dogs, muted browns and yellows and blues. Many of the shops on this block were bars selling potato beer or raw dough shops where a working dog could get a bellyful of gene-tailored yeast mash that would ferment into ethanol over the course of the day. Fra always said that he could tell when a dog was drunk by the stink of its breath, but then Fra held that most dogs were drunk most of the time.

Gio had no problem with the way dogs smelled. Even the odor of the potty pods built around the trees lining the Spaceway didn't offend him. He picked a tree with a dense infestation of posters stuck to its trunk and squatted on the stone curb of the pod to scan the ads. There were two and three sheets atop each other at a dog's eye level, but the coverage higher up was thinner and less weather beaten. He saw familiar notices for wet nurses and ear sculptors and pack cheerleaders. A tongue reduction clinic on Broad Street was offering free consultations and a disobedience group for jittery retrievers was accepting new members. Signups were open for Blackdoor's annual 5K lure course. Meat prizes for the first fifty finishers! Finally he found what he'd been looking for.

Rehearsals Are Now Underway for
The Antic Tour of Interspecies Marvels
A Scofflaw Circus!
Dogs & Cats & Humans
As You've Never Seen Them!

This was the poster which had first appeared two days ago, not only here in Puppytown but in other wards as well. Earlier versions had announced that "The Antic Tour" was "coming soon." Now the policedogs were looking to question anyone seen distributing them, but the culprits proved elusive. The posters had sparked intense comment, not only in the wards but in the galleries of the Senate itself. Like most, Gio had never heard the word *scofflaw* before. He'd learned that a scofflaw was "a person who flouts the law, especially by failing to comply with a law that is difficult to enforce effectively." And a *circus* was "a traveling company of upsider acrobats, trained animals, and clowns that gives performances, typically in a large tent, in a series of different places." Scholars at the Academy confirmed that such traditional entertainment cooperatives were native to various of the Thousand Worlds. Hali had gone to several when she was living on Franks. None had ever been seen on Boon.

What everyone wanted to know, from the high clones of Grand Houses to the catnip-addled scavengers in Sleeper Park, was this: what laws might this unknown circus flout? Interactions among dogs and cats and humans were limited by common sense, not by legislation. No self-respecting citizen of Boon would think of having sex with a different species and, although dogs and cats had their own unique challenges, all enjoyed equivalent rights with human citizens—in theory, at least. Why there was even a seat for cloned cats in the Senate, even though the grands of Macska House were not entitled to vote. Still, with all the fights—don't call them riots!—that had been breaking out around the city, relations between the species were a hot topic.

"Been to the New Forest lately, Senator?" A spaniel popped onto the curb beside Gio.

"Excuse me?" He leaned back to get a look at the dog. "Do I know you?" He was wearing the wide blue fight scarf of Gio's lawnball team, the Gogos, with the number thirty-seven in electric yellow.

KING OF THE DOGS, QUEEN OF THE CATS

"Guess."

Rust colored fur curled tight against its torso and its big ears flopped like wings when Gio scratched the dog's head in greeting. "I have a friend named Liffy. You look like you could've been from the same litter and you're wearing his number. Did he send you?"

"Maybe." He lifted a leg and peed into the ceramic pod. "Maybe not. But pretend I'm your little doggie pal."

Gio wondered why his friend needed a double, especially one with such a jangly attitude. "You've been watching me."

Fake Liffy gave him a sneering yip.

Gio surveyed the street. "Okay, what about the New Forest?" If he'd hadn't seen this dog following him, what else had he missed?

The spaniel pressed the flush pedal with his walking glove. "Not a place most senators go, but we hear you're not most senators." A jet of water washed across the potty.

Dogs were always telling him things. "So worth a look?" He kept his voice low. "Nature as I've never seen it?"

"Positively antic, if you can keep a secret." With a flip of its stubby tail, the spaniel swaggered off to the nearest bar.

REHEARSAL

The Villa Barbaro had ancient history with the New Forest, dating back to the founding of the Supremacy. Pao Barbaro had won a great victory here at the Battle of Cragon Landing. If you believed the monuments erected to honor the original Barbaro, first of all Gio's grandclones, a band of some two thousand freedom-loving humans and their uplifted servants had overrun the Cragon Collective's outpost in the year 207. This was the turning point in the war to free the colony on Boon from the corrupt upsider trading concern that had subsidized its founding. Pao had razed the Cragon spaceport and ordered that trees be planted to return the land to wilderness. Historians unsympathetic to the Villa

Barbaro after its fall from power now claimed the Battle of Cragon Landing had been a massacre. Bloody Pao had taken no prisoners and had left the bodies to rot as warning to those upsiders still at large on Boon as he formed the new government he called the Supremacy. Later he had planted the New Forest to cover up this brutal crime. Whether this was true or not—Fra was skeptical, Gio convinced—the battle had marked the beginning of Boon's two centuries of isolation from the Thousand Worlds of the upside. It had only been in the lifetime of old Pry Ullo, current leader of the Supremacy, that space-faring trade had been re-established.

The crumbling remains of the Cragon roads were the easiest way to penetrate the forest. Its canopy was mostly crown-branching evergreens, beneath which a scatter of hardy copperbark and other hardwoods reached toward the sun. The understory was dense enough to discourage exploration with its tangle of prickers and shrub fern and stink lilies. After hiking for half an hour, Gio began to wonder what he was doing. The New Forest was some seven thousand hectares, and didn't people disappear in it all the time? Did Liffy expect him to stumble on the mysterious circus all by himself when the policedogs hadn't tracked it down? When his right foot began to hurt, he sat down, pulled his shoe off and shook a pebble from it. As he stared back at the way he had come, rehearsing in his mind all the turns he had taken, he realized that he wasn't sure how to get back.

Messaging 1/34/498 Time 1152

Fra: You listen to me, Gio, I've already got a houseful for the 1230 tour. Where are you? Acknowledge, you selfish little twit. You have twenty-eight…twenty-seven minutes to get your lazy ass back here. You hear me?

End Session 1/34/498 Time 1153

So an ugly family reunion loomed at the end of this misbegotten adventure. No surprise.

A cat slithered free of the underbrush. It walked upright like a human, with knees that bent forward, unlike any other cat on Boon. It was unnaturally tall at a meter and half and beneath a stylish red doublet, it had rusty striped fur. A black top hat perched between its ears.

"Lost your way, have you?" it said.

"Not sure," Gio rose, expecting it to rub up against him. "Since I don't know where I'm going."

Instead of the traditional feline greeting, the cat took its hat off and glanced inside. "May I be of assistance?" It set the hat back on its head.

"Maybe." If Liffy had wanted him to find the circus, this must be his guide. But when did dogs trust cats with their secrets?

"I see you're travelling from the Enlightened City," said the cat. "Seeking diversion, are you? Amusement? Sights as yet unseen?"

"I was expecting a dog." He felt a riffle of doubt. This was what he'd come for, but was it what he wanted?

"There will be dogs."

At first Gio thought it was smiling, but then the smile became a yawn that was so big that he could see the rows of carnassial molars at the back of the cat's mouth.

"This way, Senator," it said.

Gio was instantly suspicious. Fra liked to say that any offer to help was an ask in disguise. That had proved true not only in the Senate, but often with humans in general. This odd creature seemed more like a human than a cat. But how could he turn away after coming this far? Especially since the circus was expecting him?

The cat encouraged him to push through what he'd thought was a solid hedge of prickers but which parted after some poking and scrabbling to reveal another broken Cragon road. She announced that her name was Scratch and that they were just a few kilometers away.

"Away from what?"

"Answers." Scratch set off. "Marvels."

Gio hurried to catch up. "You're not from Boon."

"No."

He picked a thorny twig from his sleeve. "From where, then?"

Scratch raised a foreleg—no, clearly it was an arm— and pointed to the upside without missing a step. Gio noticed that she was barehanded, but that made sense if she'd been altered to walk upright. It occurred to him that this might be a kidnapping, but he could not think of a reason why anyone would kidnap the junior of a fallen house like Villa Barbaro. "How long have you been on Boon?"

"Not long."

"And this stunt is your idea? The circus?"

"My services were called for. I'm the ringmaster."

"Called for?"

"All answers in time." The cat's tail stretched upright, with just the slightest curl at the tip. "Ssssh!" She hissed. "Can you hear it yet?"

"Hear what?"

"The music."

Gio strained to listen. Nothing. He puzzled over this strange creature as they continued. Everyone on Boon knew that dogs and cats could hear at distances many times that of humans. But if Scratch was from one of the Thousand Worlds, maybe she hadn't had much experience with humans. They trudged on in silence for another fifteen minutes before Gio could make out the groan of a distant organ.

He didn't recognize the jaunty music.

The circus had set up on an old landing pad. The concrete was fractured, making the surface a puzzle of tilted plates that approximated flatness. Weeds poked through the larger cracks. Someone had swept piles of forest litter here and there, but had yet to dispose of them. One low single-story fabric structure was completed, and another much larger structure was under construction. Gio was thrilled to see bots weaving it. Intelligent machines had been all but banned since Pao's time, rejected as the worst of the corrosive technologies from the Thousand Worlds. After all, the uplifted needed jobs to do. He counted three cats and four dogs on the odd devices arrayed around the pad. All were barehanded. Gio and Scratch approached three towers connected by nets and swings. A cat and a dog were crossing on all fours from one tower to another on a slack rope ten meters above them. It was a stout rope, thick as Gio's arm, but the two aerialists were so close together that the dog's muzzle brushed the cat's tail. They moved in perfect synchronicity, the cat calling steps as the dog mirrored its partner. Gio got a crick in his neck watching them. He felt dizzy, as if it were the planet that were tilted and not just the launch pad. This might be the most amazing thing he'd ever seen.

"Look over there." Scratch pointed.

A cat backflipped off the third tower, clearing two flaming lawnball hoops, to splash into a swimming pool. A dog immediately followed it with a nosedive, almost landing atop the cat as it paddled out of the way.

"Tomorrow, we mount a saddle on that dog," she said. "Zook will ride her down." Her voice changed register. "A death defying plunge," she announced, "through three fiery hoops." She held both arms up as if to invite applause and her pretty pink tongue swiped at her lips in delight.

But Gio was distracted by a woman and a dog who were assaulting each other on a raised stage. One would do a brief flailing dance and then slap the other with what looked like a fish. Then they would politely pass the fish to receive the same insult. Both the woman's and the dog's faces had been painted white. The dog wore a conical hat and the woman a purple wig.

"What is all this?" said Gio.

"Practice for the show," said the cat. "Do you like it?"

"Yes." How long had he been nodding? "Very much." He forced himself to stop. "But it feels dangerous."

"Dangerous how?" The cat's ears pricked.

"You know, because of the way things are." Gio thought that maybe she didn't know about the tensions between the species, so he gestured at the woman and the dog. "All right then, why are those two fighting?"

"Let's ask. Kly!"

As soon as he heard her name, Gio recognized the woman, who waved to them.

"Bring the fish," Scratch called.

Not only was Kly the junior clone of Gamane House, but she was one of the senators who had missed the import fee consensus that morning. So her absence was explained, if not excused. Kly had come of age just a few months before and had replaced Chu Gamane in the Senate; for some time Kly's forlorn senior had rarely been sober enough to attend to her senatorial duties. Gio was happy that Kly had taken over the Gamane seat because it meant that he was no longer the youngest Senator. He'd wanted to know her better but she was so new that he'd spoken to her in private just the once.

Messaging 1/34/498 Time 1238

Hali: I don't know when I've seen him like this. Are you there? He's boiling over, barely able to speak his lines on the tour. Gio? I hope whatever you're doing is worth it.

End Session 1/34/498 Time 1238

The dog who trotted beside Kly also looked familiar. "Liffy?"

"I knew you'd come, Boss." He sat and touched a paw to Gio's knee. Boss was Gio's nickname on the Gogos because he called plays for the defense. Liffy was his star left picket.

"Wasn't sure with all that makeup. Plus you lent your fight scarf to that mutt in town." Gio held out a hand to Kly. "Hello, Senator Gamane."

"Delighted to see you, Gio." She smiled at him as they shook hands; her teeth looked buttery against her thick white makeup. "I didn't think you'd accept the invitation. Well done!"

He blinked, unsure whether to be pleased or chagrined. Who was this woman to be having opinions about him?

She waved her fish at the towers. "You'll find that our show is everything the Senate is not."

"We need performers from all the peoples of Boon," said Scratch. "Especially humans." Her tail brushed Kly's back. "Especially distinguished humans."

Kly tilted her head and gave Gio a tickled look.

"You realize that the policedogs want to speak to you." Gio reminded himself that Scratch was a dangerous alien and Kly was a reckless junior. But what did that matter, really? These were the most interesting people he'd met in years. "How have you been able to keep this place a secret?"

"Oh, they know where we are, Boss," said Liffy. "All the dogs know."

"Cats too," said Scratch.

"So it's only the Senate that's in the dark?" he said.

"Along with the rest of the government." Kly smirked. "As usual."

When Gio had been a boy, if a crack like this from a Senator had gotten back to Pry Ullo, there would have been consequences. But who feared the wrath of the Supremacy now? Pry's crumbling government could barely collect the garbage, much less police opinion. Still, it was better to leave the subversive chatter here in the New Forest. As Fra liked to say, nobody ever died of caution.

"Gio wanted to know why you were fighting," said Scratch.

"Fighting?" Liffy gave a low growl. "Dogs don't fight with humans."

"He means the routine." Kly scratched Liffy between the ears, and Gio felt a pang of jealousy. "It's supposed to be funny. That's why we look this way. We're clowns." She cocked her hip and patted her purple wig. "We're deliberate exaggerations, Senator Scofflaw."

Although he was charmed by her wisecrack, he managed to suppress a smile. "Why weren't you laughing?"

"I did laugh the first time he swatted me, because I didn't expect it. That's our act. We surprise people into laughing."

"I don't get the joke."

"Let me explain," said Liffy and raised a leg as if to pee on Gio's shoe.

"Gah!" Gio reflexively skipped back but then recognized the fake as the way dogs taunted one another on his lawnball team. And yes, there was Liffy's breathy, muffled *hhuh-hhah-hhuh-hhah*, which was how dogs laughed. "Ha-ha yourself, mutt."

"Surprise is the key," said Kly. "As well as being improper without giving offense." She offered Gio the fish with mock solemnity and he was so surprised that he accepted it. The thing looked real but was made of some synthetic that flopped convincingly. It felt wet to the touch.

"I think he gets it now," said Liffy.

The diving dog and cat, having defied death for the last time that day, scrambled out of the pool. The dog shook water in every direction and Zook squatted on her haunches and began to groom herself dry with her tongue. A bare-chested commoner in orange and blue striped pants sprayed the hoops with a hose, dousing the flame.

"I hear you're a friend to dogs," said Kly. "I'm a cat person myself. That's what the show is about." Grinning, she spread arms wide, as if to embrace the entire planet. "We're just one big happy family."

The circus felt like something Gio had always wanted, even though he hadn't known it until now. He had to believe that they'd lured him here for a reason. But joining up would mean nothing but trouble for someone in his position. He couldn't—*shouldn't*—decide his future on an impulse. Fra would be outraged; he'd say mingling like this with lesser citizens was beneath their dignity. And sickly Pry Ullo had an abiding suspicion of upsiders and their egalitarian politics, even though he desperately needed their cloning technology. No, he mustn't let them rush him. Gio could lose his seat in the Senate, his home, his family. He wished the cat would hurry up and make her offer. Then he could tell her he'd have to think about it and make his escape. Not that he was looking forward to the long night of accusation and argument that awaited him back at the villa.

Scratch tipped her hat off to check inside again. "But look at the time," she said, as if reading his mind. "You'll be wanting to leave us. It's a long walk back." She put it back on.

This abrupt dismissal took him aback. They were just sending him away?

"I'll take you," said Liffy. "Just let me get cleaned up."

Had he said something to offend Scratch? Maybe she'd decided that he was useless to them. Glumly, Gio watched Liffy trot toward the smaller of the two tents. And why hadn't Kly offered to take him back to the city? When he thought about how excited he'd been just a moment before, he felt foolish.

Kly touched his arm. "You won't tell anybody about us?"

He could see a rim of creamy brown skin around her eyes at the edge of the ridiculous white makeup. "Seems like half the Enlightened City knows already." He tried to picture her in her Senatorial sash. "Who's left to tell?"

"Your senior," she said. "Mine. Other senators. Ullo House and their agents. Sure, they all know we're somewhere in the forest. But they don't know why we're here."

"Neither do I." He heard the edge to his voice. A wasted afternoon was about to give way to an angry evening. "But I'll come to your show," he said. "That is, if they don't arrest you first."

"Nobody is getting arrested," said the cat. "The show opens soon."

Gio doubted that. "This is yours." He held out the fish to them.

Kly turned it away. "No, you keep it."

"Compliments of the Antic Tour of Interspecies Marvels," said Scratch.

Kly took a deep bow. "A scofflaw circus."

He was tempted to tell her about the attack on the statue of her grand to pierce her self-assurance. But no, they were right, it was time for him to go. "I can't be walking around the city carrying a fish." He was annoyed with these silly and insistent people. "A fake fish made who knows where. The upside, that's for sure."

Liffy had raced back carrying a sports duffle between his teeth, once again the familiar spaniel Gio knew. His reddish brown fur was damp and he was wearing stylish leather walking gloves and the Gogo's yellow and blue fight collar. He looked like he'd just come off a lawn. Gio realized then that Liffy's double in Oldgate would give him an alibi in case agents of the Supremacy got suspicious.

Liffy dropped the duffle at Gio's feet. "Better put that in here with your pads and your jersey." He smiled. "Nice practice today, Boss, but it's time to trot."

HUMANS

Gio never liked eating in Villa Barbaro's Olympus Salon. As a child, he'd been distracted by the frescoes. On the high ceiling a gaggle of gods and goddesses lounged on clouds. Their clothes were falling off, revealing swaths of pale flesh. On the walls, fading trompe-l'œil doors and windows opened onto busy scenes of the First World with people riding horses and unloading ships bobbing at anchor. The painted folk had paid no attention to the lonely boy who longed to leap through the imaginary windows into their lost world. Listening to Fra boast about the grandeur of the Barbaros through dinner after dinner as leaks from the ceiling dribbled into vases and the bits of mural peeled from the walls, Gio had resolved to escape someday, not only from the Villa Barbaro but from Boon itself. Maybe he'd never see the First World, but he could at least become an upsider.

Recently, however, what bothered him were the images of the original owners, the Barbaros and their families, dead these fifteen centuries. The artist had rendered them with fierce verisimilitude, and unlike the gods, they stared brazenly down at Gio from their faux balcony. Husbands and wives, servants and children, even pets, a green parrot and a little dog, watched him slurp noodles and fork dumplings. He couldn't escape the suspicion that they were judging him.

Hali understood his discomfort. She often joked that the chilly atmosphere of the Olympus Salon worked better for her than any diet.

Nobody spoke during dinner. At a less fraught meal, they might've chatted about the day's events. Fra would've let Hali play recorded music, as long as she kept it to a murmur. But tonight the senior was in an evil mood. Whenever there was trouble in the family, he insisted on finishing the meal in silence before the fireworks were served. So they ate in punishing solitude, each clink of cutlery on china like a shout.

KING OF THE DOGS, QUEEN OF THE CATS

It wasn't until they'd finished their pie and kahve was being poured that Fra spoke. "Clear these plates away," he said to the two dogs serving them, "and leave us."

Colpi bowed. Their ancient servant was almost as dilapidated as the house. He was a traditionalist and insisted on walking on two legs when serving them. Uplifted dogs could walk upright, but even with enhanced hind and forelegs, they were more at ease on all fours. Prolonged standing was tiring for even the youngest pup, and Colpi was old at a doddering twenty-seven. Hali and Gio thought he should retire, but he resisted and Fra didn't have the heart to force the issue. Fra's grand, Kao, had brought Colpi to the Villa Barbaro when he was just a pup. The aged dog closed all four doors, clumping around the salon as if his paws and hands had turned to stone. Then they were alone.

"Eight hours." Fra set his cup down on a mismatched saucer, careful to turn the chip in the rim away from him. It was an heirloom that dated from the building of the villa. The rest of the set had been lost or broken by clumsy servants over the centuries. Fra only asked for it when he was under stress. "You left me here with dogs and cats and citizens for eight hours."

"Dogs and cats are citizens," said Hali. "And I was here too."

He flicked fingers at her. "You didn't have to give tours."

"Showing the house is your job." She gazed down her nose at him. "Keeping it is mine."

"Your job is to be my wife."

"And Gio's."

Let them bicker. Gio knew they'd turn on him soon enough.

"We were worried about you." Hali turned to Gio. "With all that's been going on. And then Leeol's statue…"

Fra interrupted. "Where were you?"

"Out."

"Out is not a place. It's an evasion."

"…and then that statue was bombed." Hali intended to be heard, even if it annoyed Fra. "And the feeds keep chattering about missing dogs and cats. And a grand too. That Gamane girl, Chu's junior. What's her name? Cry?"

"Kly." Fra was irritated to be arguing with his wife instead of scolding his clone. "The girl's name was Kly."

"Was?" Hali pressed both hands to the table, alarmed. "Not is? What have you heard?"

All this talk of Kly struck Gio as risky, so he changed the subject. "After the consensus was postponed," he said, "I thought I'd go to practice." He'd concocted an account of his day that didn't include a visit to the New Forest. "I was cutting through the plaza when the paintbomb went off."

"And that's when I told you to come home."

It had been Liffy's idea. "You told me that you wanted me for the twelve-thirty tour. There was plenty of time for a scrimmage, so I called my pal Liffy and some others. And afterward, okay, yes, I went out with a couple of my dogs for a mug of snooker." He shook his head, trying to look repentant. "Maybe more than one mug."

"Practice? You went to practice?"

"For his lawnball team," said Hali.

"*I know he plays lawnball.*" Fra shouted. Everyone in the villa heard him, as did half the grands in the neighborhood. He lowered his voice. "We've been to the games, Hal." He unfolded his napkin, then refolded it. "What's wrong with you tonight?"

"I was worried about him." Hali rubbed her forehead. "About that statue and the bomb and then he didn't answer. Bad things happen, especially these days." She was mumbling now, so that Gio had to lean in to hear her. "Or maybe I'm just being silly." She made eye contact with Gio. Was that a wink? She wouldn't dare. "But now he's here." Her tone brightened. "Safe with us."

He realized that she was deflecting Fra's wrath onto herself. She knew her husbands and their tempers. Gio had been ready to meet Fra's fire with his own, but she was offering a way to retreat, at least from this battle. All he had to do was make the bully believe he'd won.

"Your first call came while I was on the field," Gio said. "The second...I admit I didn't answer. I knew I couldn't get back in time and I was embarrassed. That was selfish of me."

"I called you *three* times."

"I swear I only got two." Gio had ignored two but hadn't received the third. Was that because the feed didn't reach the New Forest? Maybe the lost call was Scratch's doing. "Must have been some malfunction," he said, knowing it was the perfect excuse. The technology they could afford often proved unreliable. "I'll take my ear-stone in to have it checked." He sucked in a breath. "Look, Fra, I'm sorry you had to do both tours today." Actually, Gio was only on the schedule for the 1530 tour; the 1230 was Fra's. But Gio would let that go and stuff his pride into his pocket. "I'll do all three tours tomorrow, okay? You take the day off. Go to the Senate and make your speech."

"Good for you." Hali reached to pat Gio's hand. "Very diplomatic, dear." Without letting go of Gio, she caught Fra's hand as well. "I like it when my boys work their differences out. Like the senators they are."

Fra was already subsiding. "Apology accepted," he said. "I know that our nature can be troublesome at times."

What was it that the dogs said about him? All bark and no bite.

ANTIC

The original Villa Barbaro had been designed for two distinguished First World brothers, Daniele and Marcantonio Barbaro, who had lived together in ancient times. The architect had attached two residential wings to the central block of public rooms and the brothers moved their families into each of these two identical attached apartments. The hallway on the second floor of the apartments stretched from the end of one wing through Olympus all the way to the end of the other. It was designed so that when the original Barbaros were feeling fraternal they could open doors and see the entire length of their villa.

That night, every door in Gio's wing was closed.

JAMES PATRICK KELLY

His study was the southernmost of the ten shabby rooms on the two levels of his half of the villa. It was as far away from the public spaces and his senior as could be. Gio brooded at his desk, paying no attention to the scatter of paperwork on it: minutes of meetings he was happy to forget and drafts of perpetually amended legislation that would never pass. He replayed the argument with Fra, alternating between relief and frustration. The acid that had crept up his throat at dinner had settled back into his gut, now that he was protected behind seven closed doors. He wasn't ready for an immediate breakup with Fra, but he didn't see how to avoid one. He couldn't keep giving in to that bully. Or could he? Should he move out? How would he live? It was a bad time to be taking chances, with Ullo House losing its grip on the Supremacy and no clear succession plan. Meanwhile, all the three species were in an uproar. The bombing that morning was just the latest incident. The other Grand Houses were nervous about cats seeking more privilege and dogs agitating to catch up to the cats. Gio thought that if the uplifted animals ever united to make common cause, the entire government might well collapse, especially if they found out that the supply of clones had dwindled and there was as yet no way to replace them. But were the Barbaros positioned to replace the Ullos as the Supreme House? Maybe if Gio had cared as much about politics as he did about running away to join the circus.

Thinking about the circus calmed Gio down. He wondered how they'd set those hoops on fire. Imagine the size of the crowds that flaming hoops on lawnball pitches would draw! He chuckled, then remembered that silly fish they had given him. He retrieved Liffy's duffle from his bedroom and brandished the fish like a sword as he returned to the study. It sagged into a lazy "C" and he chuckled again, his mood improving. The thing was quite marvelous. How could it feel moist but leave his hands dry? He keyed his armoire open. The fish would make an excellent addition to his collection.

Messaging 1/34/498 Time 2204

Kly: Don't you be going to bed. We need to talk.

Gio: How did you get my access?

Kly: Ways. Let me in.

Gio: Where are you?

Kly: I can see a light in the last window, second floor. That's you, right?

Gio: What do you want?

Kly: You'll find out. Which way? Don't want your senior to see me.

Gio: This is so wrong.

Kly: And?

Gio: Go through the middle arch, my side of the colonnade.

End Session 1/34/498 Time 2206

He met her at the foot of his private stairs, yanked her through the door and locked it.

"Did you miss me?" She was wearing a black cape with a hood that covered her hair and drooped almost to her eyes. She looked like a spy escaped from some historical thriller about the Broken Years after the expulsion of the Cragons.

"What are you playing at, Kly?"

"The future." Even in the gloom of the stairway, he could see her smile. "Mine. Yours, if you're lucky." She poked him. "Invite me in."

He led her up the steps to the second floor landing. As they passed through dark and empty rooms, he saw his villa through her eyes: the brown stains on the plaster, broken floor tiles in the abandoned sun salon, spider webs dangling from the eaves. He led her past the music room with the antique freeboard that nobody could play and the library which had been stripped of much of its collection, the rarest books having been sold to pay for maintenance of the public rooms. Kly seemed amused by the care with which he opened and closed doors to his forlorn chambers so as not to disturb the rest of the house. She lingered as they passed through his bedroom, her attention caught by the massive four poster bed with its sagging canopy. She ran a hand along the chenille bedspread.

"Purple?" she said.

"Hali calls it tulip. She's the one who chose it."

She stretched her arms out and let herself drop backwards onto the bed. "She must like her space." Her hood fell away from her face. "Though it's a bit of a reach over to your side when the mood hits her." She gazed across her body at him, an eyebrow arched. "Or doesn't she visit you here?"

"This way." Gio opened the door to his study.

Kly rolled to her feet. "Wait." She noticed the rumpled daybed in the corner. "Who sleeps there? The dog?"

"I do. Can we get this over with?"

As they entered the study, she noticed the fish on the middle shelf of the armoire. "You kept it!" She gave a cry of delight. "Scratch said you'd like it."

Before he could stop her, she was admiring his collection.

"Look at all this wonderful…" She hesitated. "…stuff."

"Not stuff." He eased the bedroom door shut. "Curiosities." He hurried over. "Please don't touch."

"Does this thing work?" She pointed to the translator, a dented ball microphone mounted on a squat processor box that Hali had given him when he was a boy.

"It's supposed to translate Cragon tradespeech but no. Won't wake up. We think it was Pao's."

"Is that dirt?" She nodded at his rack of test tubes.

"Sand. From beaches on the Thousand Worlds."

"Which ones."

"Ter Quan," he said. "Jack's Store. That one is from Kenning, where the High Gregorys live."

"How do you know that?" She looked suspicious. "You've never been off Boon."

"I have contacts at the new spaceport. We trade. An engineer on the *State of Grace* had maybe fifty of these."

"And this knobby thing? Looks broken."

"Ahh…" He cleared his throat. "Actually, I swiped that. When my Senate committee toured the *Black Sun* last year, I noticed that it had fallen into a corner of the communications pod. Like you said, it's broken so they were going to have to replace…"

KING OF THE DOGS, QUEEN OF THE CATS

"Wait, is that Exotic?" She peered at the ceramic shard with its tessellated spiral flower pattern that was the prize of his collection of upsider artifacts. The lost civilization called the Exotics had created the wormholes connecting the Thousand Worlds.

Pride puffed him up. "From the ruins on Sanctuary."

"So, a fan of the upside. Interesting." Kly dragged herself away from the collection to survey the rest of his study. "A daring hobby for a grand, I'd say. And costly." She sauntered past his desk, glancing at the paperwork. "Did Pao leave treasure we don't know about?"

"No law against bartering for artifacts from the Thousand Worlds. And we had eighteen landings last year, up from just five in 494." Gio locked the armoire. "The more traffic, the more chances for bargains. Pry Ullo keeps authorizing new trading licenses. He may hate upsiders, but he loves the landing fees."

"To save up so that he can replace that old somatic cell transfer lab."

Gio was speechless at her careless mention of the looming clone crisis, the most serious threat the Supremacy had ever faced.

She appeared not to notice. "And you two Barbaros serve on the Customs subcommittee. That must help."

She continued around the room, touching his things as if shopping: the hourglass, his all-star plate, the dusty fronds of a potted alamy tree. "I'm beginning to understand why she was so interested when I mentioned you, Gio." Kly unfastened her cape and folded it over the arm of the couch.

"She?"

"Scratch." Kly tossed a throw pillow aside and sat.

"Is that what this is about?" Gio faced her, leaning against his desk.

"Why, what do you imagine is about to happen, Senator Barbaro?"

"Either you want me to join the circus. Or you're flirting."

"You'll know when I start flirting." She smirked.

"I'm married, Kly."

"Half married. But leave that for now." She fixed him with an intense gaze. "We need grands, Gio. I'm the only one so far. Your support could be important."

"Why? It's a show, Kly."

"Some will see a show. Some will see another way for the species to get along."

"If you're offering me a spot, I'm definitely interested. I won't deny it. But no advocating." He stabbed a hand at

KING OF THE DOGS, QUEEN OF THE CATS

her to keep her from interrupting. "I can't speak for the Barbaros. It wouldn't be fair to Fra. Not to mention that he'd kill me."

"Speak for yourself then. I don't speak for my house."

"It's a bad time." She had to know that the Senate galleries were buzzing with dire news. Dogs walking off the job. Cats organizing. Rumors of conspiracies. All relatively peaceful—so far. "The political situation…"

"Makes this the perfect time. Pry Ullo is too sick and his junior Den is too timid to hold the Supremacy. Boon is changing."

"Another house will take their place, and squash anyone who gets in their way." A thought occurred to him. "Maybe your senior would like it to be the Gamanes?"

She gave him an acid grin. "Chu's a useless drunk and I'm going my own way. We're like the Barbaros. A house divided."

They both seemed shocked to hear the particular truth spoken aloud. "You don't know that." Gio didn't like the way she kept prodding him for a reaction.

She was silent for a long moment, considering her next move. "You heard about today's paintbomb?" she said finally. "Old Leeol defaced?"

"Your great-grand? I was there."

Kly rested her head against the back of the couch. "I did that."

"*What?*" The back of his neck tingled.

"Traitor to my own house." Was she talking to the ceiling? The Thousand Worlds? "Nobody else knows." She made it sound like an achievement.

"Why?" He sank onto the chair behind his desk.

"A gesture to free myself. From my senior. From the Supremacy." She shook herself. "From history."

"Did Scratch tell you to do that?"

"You don't listen." She shook her head. 'I told you, nobody knows. Nobody but you."

Did he believe that? He wanted to, but was her trust in telling him a compliment or a trap? "What does that cat want?" he said. "Really?"

"Where she comes from everyone has equal rights."

"Right, and they live on clouds and dance with rainbows."

Silence.

"We have equal rights," he said, but the words seemed to twist in his mouth. "You know, within reason."

"*Equivalent* rights." Her mocking laugh stung him. "Not the same as equal."

KING OF THE DOGS, QUEEN OF THE CATS

"Rights given their abilities," he said. "We're different from dogs and cats. Different senses, different bodies, different brains."

"The only difference that counts?" she said. "When humans tell them what to do, they have to do it. We treat them like children, Gio."

Arguing with her felt like arguing with himself. "You can't deny there's a difference in intelligence…"

"Didn't you read my report for the Committee on Species Amity?" She shot off the couch, her face flushed with anger. "Take a dog and a human with the exact same score on the upsiders' Intelligence Complex." She tossed papers around his desk, searching. "Scientists bring test subjects to the lab, citizens of all species. Test subjects interview the dog and the human for an hour. Then they interview the subjects." She found the report she was looking for, folded to the right page and read. "Eighty-two percent of the humans say the human was more intelligent than the dog. What's worse is that fifty-two percent of the dogs say the same thing." She dropped the report in front of him. "But the dog and the human have the same scores. Identical IC."

Gio flipped back to the cover. "Who says this?"

With two quick steps Kly was at the armoire. "Studies, Gio. Plural. That's just the latest. Submitted by the Academy of the Thousand Worlds." She punctuated *Thousand* and *Worlds* with a knock on the cabinet sharp enough to rattle his collection.

"Not so loud." He guided her back to the couch and she let herself be led. "So what are you, one of those who claim it was a crime to uplift them and not make them as smart as us? Cruel to make them grow hands and walk on hind legs? That all happened a long time ago, and believe me, the dogs and cats I know are happy to be alive."

"I know that. But the point is, they deserve our respect." She sat and then pulled him down onto the couch next to her. "Why don't we have bots, Senator? You and I? Cats and dogs?"

He frowned. "What does that have to do with anything?"

"The Ullos have bots. A few of the other grand houses do too. Anyone should be able to have bots, except that old Pry Ullo says no."

Fra had always wanted a bot, but had never been able to afford one. Gio spouted the official line while he considered the real reason. "We'll get more of them as we develop our infrastructure. And we need to manage the economic impacts." He was hearing Fra's voice come out of his mouth. "Can't be putting dogs and cats out of work."

KING OF THE DOGS, QUEEN OF THE CATS

It was hard to say things to her that he knew weren't true but he still hadn't decided whether to trust her.

"Did we ask them if they like doing jobs that bots could do? Pry Ullo and his government aren't afraid of technology, they're afraid of the changes it will bring. Your dog pals might like to try some new lines of work. Have the same chances we have. "

He held up hands in surrender. "And your circus will make that happen?"

"It'll make everyone think. It's making you think."

"I've already been thinking," he said irritably.

"Really? Have you ever had a conversation like this with anyone?"

"No." He sighed. "How about you?"

"With some cats. The dogs at the circus." Her voice dropped to a whisper. "You're the only human." Then she kissed him.

Her lips were soft and hot. His were hard at first but then they weren't. She pulled away before he did.

"Was that Scratch's idea or yours?" His voice was a stone in his throat.

"Mine." There was no hesitation. "And it was a good one. So tell me, are you happy being a Barbaro?"

He swallowed. "What else would I be?"

She grinned and pulled him to his feet.

Gio was surprised that sex with Kly wasn't that great. She certainly filled the eye and she was enthusiastic. And it took no time at all for him to respond to her restless hands. But there was an awkwardness to the way their bodies tangled, as if they had grown extra knees. Some of their foreplay felt more like debating than caressing. And then he was remembering how she'd called Hali his half wife. For a moment he lost his way, but Kly came to their rescue by squirming on top of him. He'd had other lovers before. So had Fra and Hali. So why couldn't he just enjoy Kly the way she seemed to be enjoying him? If only she weren't making so much noise. Even though all the doors were closed, he imagined Fra bursting in on them. In the end, he pretended to have an orgasm, so they could stop and he could figure out what was happening.

She rolled off him and pulled the sheets up, leaving the chenille bedspread bunched at the foot of the enormous bed that he rarely used. Neither spoke as their breathing subsided. Then her hand found his. "I don't know about you, but first time is never the charm for me."

Gio's eyes went wide. "Really." He tried to imagine what charming might look like on this woman. "I couldn't tell."

She squeezed his hand. "Don't take that wrong. You were great. It's just that I get to thinking too hard with a new lover. Wondering. Planning."

"Planning?"

"What to do next time, you know."

Despite his disappointment, he liked the idea of a next time. "So I fit into your plans?"

There was music in her laugh that he hadn't heard before. "You can be funny when you want."

The compliment made him want to kiss her, so he did. "I can do better too," he whispered into her mouth. "Less thinking next time. Promise."

He felt her smile, then she pushed him away. "Good. Now that we agree on an agenda, I've got to get home. I bet there are policedogs searching for me."

He watched as she scuttled around the room gathering the clothes he'd tugged off her.

"By the way...," she said, as she shimmied into her slacks, "...you're my alibi for today. We've been having hot sex all over the Enlightened City like the pair of depraved grands that we are."

"I already have an alibi," he said. "I was playing lawnball."

"Now you have two." She headed for the door.

"Wait."

She paused with her hand on the knob. "Don't worry, I won't make a sound."

"No. What about the show?"

"The show must go on. With or without you." She blew him a kiss. "Talk later."

TOUR

What Gio dreaded even more than school groups of cats were school groups that mixed kittens and puppies and children. There was no keeping them from teasing and then squabbling. He was all for teaching proper species socialization but not while he was giving the tours that subsidized the upkeep of their historic estate. Neither Fra nor Gio relished these daily invasions, but to pay their bills, the grands of the Villa Barbaro were forced to welcome tourists into their home and to show them the sights.

He met his visitors in the knot garden in front of the main house. Of the three daily tours, the 0900 was usually the least crowded. This one included six advanced learners on a field trip from the Respectful Friendship

Alliance: two kittens, four puppies and a shy six-year-old girl. They were chaperoned by a pair of teachers—human and cat—and two dog parents. Also waiting was a dog family consisting of a mother, a father, and a bored adolescent, and a wide-eyed human couple who looked like they had just come from mucking out a barn. A tour of sixteen was no problem, but at 0901, just as Gio was ushering them toward the colonnade, Scratch strolled up.

"Is this the tour?" she said. "Sorry I'm late."

Everybody gawked at this odd upright creature, almost as tall as an adult human but unmistakably feline. One of the puppies growled and said to no one in particular, "His legs go the wrong way,"

"Hush," said the cat teacher.

"I'm a she." Scratch stooped to the crushed gravel path to pet the puppy. He gave a panicky bark, backed up three steps and sat down. "Where I come from there are lots of cats and dogs like me."

The kittens were brazen, as cats so often were. A calico bunted against Scratch's legs, using the scent glands in its chin to greet her. The others followed. "I like your hat," said the calico.

"Did I miss the introductions?" She chucked a kitten under the chin. "I'm Scratch."

KING OF THE DOGS, QUEEN OF THE CATS

Gio had grown roots, his thoughts wooden. What was this upsider doing?

"Where are you from, Scratch?" The cat teacher's tail switched curiously back and forth.

"The circus," she said. "I'm the ringmaster."

"Circus?" One of the humans, who Gio decided must be farmers on a visit to the city, scowled at her wife, who shrugged.

Although Scratch's evasion filled Gio with dread, the rest of the tour were thrilled. They crowded her with breathless questions and declarations. *When is the show— my mom says it's funny—can puppies go—is it scary—are cats in charge—are you really a cat—who's in it—is it too loud— what does it cost—I don't like loud—I heard scary funny—loud is fun—will the policedogs be there?*

Scratch stopped them. "My friends, we're here to see the Villa Barbaro. Maybe we should let the senator show us his house."

The little ones squirmed with disappointment but the chaperones enforced order.

Then everyone was staring at Gio.

"Welcome, all." He had to collect himself. "My name is Gio Barbaro and I am a clone of the original owner of this house, Pao Barbaro." He focused on the puppies as the least threatening members of his audience. "Who knows who that is?"

They all did, of course.

"And what do you know about him?" Gio waited. "Anyone?"

"Scary," blurted one of the bolder puppies, a terrier.

The little girl chimed in. "Fought with the mean space people."

The cat teacher corrected her. "They were called the Cragon Collective."

"Great leader," said one farmer.

"He founded the Supremacy," the other said.

"Did you ever meet him?" said the terrier.

"No," said Gio, "he died a hundred and seventy-three years ago in this very house. All right, then." He lapsed into the familiar spiel. "Although my great-great-great-grand ordered this house to be built, he did not come up with the design himself. It's a copy of another house built on the First World by an ancient architect. His name was Palladio. Now this Palladio had a friend who was a painter. His name was Veronese."

It never failed that the little ones would twitter at the funny old names. Once again, the chaperones settled them with disapproving glares.

KING OF THE DOGS, QUEEN OF THE CATS

Gio continued, gaining confidence. "Palladio asked his friend Veronese to decorate the house, so that it would become one of the most beautiful anywhere. Let's go upstairs now and see how they did."

They passed through the colonnade and up the long stairway to the second floor. Gio ushered them through Olympus. "We'll come back here in a little while, but we'll start in the formal reception rooms." He found his place in the bay at the front of the house and turned to face them. "Everybody take a moment to look around, but please, don't touch."

The puppies and cats scattered, greeting the trompe-l'œil frescos tucked into every corner of the cross-shaped space. *What are they wearing?—Over here—Not really a door—No, here—Creepy—Look, a dog—But she's flat—I found a cat—It's like we can touch her—He said don't touch—Is she a woman or a man—Before they made us smart.*

Gio noticed that the young girl hung back, clutching at the sleeve of her human teacher.

"Senator?" The mother from the dog family approached. "This is amazing. But these pictures, what do they mean?"

Gio nodded. "They're a kind of game the artist wants you to play with him." One by one, the tourists stopped burbling to listen. "He paints a fake door to fool you into believing it's a real door."

"I know that. But why?"

"First, it's a way to show his skill. Also, he's trying to save money because it's cheaper to paint fancy doors and marble columns than to pay for them." That got the usual laugh. "But it's also a way to show the owners to themselves with these scenes from their everyday life. A way of life we can scarcely imagine. Think of it as a kind of mirror where nothing can ever change."

One of the dogs nuzzled the tarp protecting a water-damaged mural, one of two in the reception suite that Fra couldn't afford to restore. "Can we look underneath this?"

The chaperone yanked her away. "He told you not to touch!"

"No, please don't," said Gio. "You see, there's a picture underneath that's sick and we're trying to make it better. But that's why we printed a copy on the coverup so you can tell what it will look like when we're done."

"I don't get it," said a farmer, "This is your house but none of the humans look like you."

"No, they're the people who hired Palladio and Veronese to build their house fifteen centuries ago. Let's step back to the Olympus Salon and I'll introduce you to the original owners."

"Too many pretend dogs," sniffed a kitten as they retraced their steps.

A puppy skittered too close to her. "Because dogs are best."

She hissed him away.

"The Barbaros definitely liked their dogs." Gio kept the group moving. "Veronese painted nine on the walls and ceilings here. And three cats."

"All kept as pets," said Scratch.

The adult dogs rumbled at this and the cat teacher's ears went flat.

It turned out that Vix, the calico kitten, had won one of the writing contests Fra sponsored to attract school field trips. More tourist traffic to the Villa Barbaro meant Fra could request an increase in the stipend from the Supremacy. Vix had her masterpiece with her, so Gio felt obligated to let her read.

She wobbled on hind legs as everyone gathered around her. "The old Villa Barbaro," she read, "was built long ago on a farm where rich humans lived."

"Some farmhouse," said one of the farmers. She was gaping open-mouthed at the vault filled with paintings of naked gods, none of whom had ever pulled a weed. "What did they grow?"

"Grapes," said Gio "Please go on, Vix."

"It's called a villa because of the place where it was built. This was near a city called Venice in a country called California, which was covered with wineyards. The humans in California didn't have houses like ours. They built giant villas all over the place with lots of rooms and when they messed up one room, they just moved to another one. They had servants to clean up after them but they weren't dogs or cats because we weren't smart back then. I would not have liked to live in those olden times but I would like to live in a villa. I hope we can visit Villa Barbaro someday to see how the rich humans on Boon live." She glanced from her paper for approval. "The end."

Scratch was the first to start clapping.

Everyone craned their necks as they listened to Gio explain the complicated frescos on the ceiling. "You can see the pantheon of gods gathered around the central figure of Divine Wisdom…"

A dizzy puppy toppled into a kitten, followed by shrieks and insults before they were separated. Gio started skipping parts of his talk to get through this ordeal.

KING OF THE DOGS, QUEEN OF THE CATS

"At the corners are personifications of the four elements, Earth, Air, Fire and Water. And in between them are smaller paintings called cameos in which you can see Love, Abundance, Luck…"

Messaging 1/35/498 Time 0932

Scratch: We need to talk. In a few moments, I'll pretend to get a message, make my excuses and leave. I'll wait down in the kitchen for you to finish the tour. I know you can't reply, but nod so I know you understand.

End Session 1/35/498 Time 0933

How did the cat get his access? No doubt the same way Kly got it. Gio swallowed his unease. He was ready to join them, so why did Kly and Scratch keep coming after him this way? He realized that saying yes wasn't enough for them. They wanted more. Something political? But he was just the junior clone of this sad old house. What good could he be to them? Nevertheless, he couldn't shake the sense that they were closing in around him.

"I said," one of the farmers was tugging at his sleeve, "there's no furniture, so what do people do in here other than stare at the ceiling?"

Gio came back to himself and, without thinking, nodded to acknowledge the woman's question. "We... my senior and my...our wife..." He shuddered as the cat took her hat off and tucked it into the crook of her arm. "Dinner, we eat...and the servants, they...they move the table and chairs in. Otherwise, with all the tours..." He gestured at the crowd with a mirthless chuckle.

"Can we go down there now?" Vix pointed down the long eastern hallway.

"No, sorry. Those are my senior's rooms." Gio turned west. "And here are mine. All off limits, I'm afraid." He imagined fleeing the tour, slamming door after door until he was locked safe in his study. "But look all the way down." He had to re-start his patter. "You'll see the life-sized painting of a man. And at the other end, a woman. The man is Veronese and the woman is his wife, Elena."

"They look like they're watching each other," said the farmer. "Did they live here too?"

"No," said Gio. "Just the Barbaro families."

"And where did Pao live?" said Scratch. "This was his idea, no? Not only this villa, but all the grand houses. The whole Supremacy system."

"The east wing." Gio pointed toward his quarters. "That was the first part closed in. He lived here while the rest of Villa Barbaro was being built because his other house had burned down."

"Torched, you mean," said a farmer. "By mad dogs."

"That's just one story," said Gio. "Some say the Cragons were responsible."

"Or that he did it himself and blamed them," said the adolescent dog. It was the first time he had spoken.

"I like how this place fits together." Scratch was gazing down into her hat. "The art and the architecture. Two wings, two brothers. And now two clones. It's beautiful, symmetry is." She fixed him with a challenging gaze that reminded him of Fra. "Wasn't it Palladio who said that a truly beautiful building was like a body where all the parts must work with each other, even the smallest, most inconsequential bit? I think the quote is something like, 'All are necessary to do what needs doing.'"

Nobody had an answer for her, least of all Gio.

Scratch licked her lips and put her hat back on. "Well then," she said. "I've just had wonderful news. We've obtained all necessary permits and with the gracious consent of Ullo House, our Antic Tour of Interspecies Marvels will open in twelve days on the West Lawns."

Puppies jumped at Scratch's shins, barking with joy, while a pair of kittens started playing a tumbling game. Several of the adult dogs yipped.

"However, I'm afraid that means I must leave you," said Scratch. "I apologize, Senator, but I must see to my performers. This is a lovely villa and you are a gracious host." She held both arms outstretched as if to embrace them all and her voice boomed. "And I expect to see all of you at the show."

The last twenty minutes of the tour were the longest of Gio's life.

MARVELS

"Ah, there you are, Gio." Hali waved as she sat across the servants' table from Scratch, while Colpi served them. The cat had her back to him, but he recognized her hat. "The Ambassador tells me that she's just come from your tour. But I understand that you didn't recognize our distinguished guest?"

"Ambassador?" Gio couldn't help himself. "Ambassador of what?"

"Apologies for not introducing myself, Senator Barbaro." Scratch rose and stretched, her spine flexing like a bow. "Mar Nacima Scratak." She strode around the table, hand extended in the traditional human greeting.

"Cultural Ambassador, representing the Nearspace Cooperative Sphere."

Gio knew that by now he should be used to these shocks but he was still taken aback. He tried to sound like a senator and not a clueless dolt. "I'm honored, Ambassador." He grasped the cat's hand, as if it might be the clue to this new mystery. "I would have prepared, had I know you'd be joining us." He'd never held a cat's hand. It was smaller than his. Her unfurled fingers were like furry bones and the broad pad on the palm was dry and hot.

Colpi approached the table carrying a tray with cups and a pot of kahve.

"Which is why I surprised you. But you must call me Scratch." Gio felt the rasp of her blunt claws against his wrist. Then she gave Gio a final reassuring squeeze and let go.

"I told you I'd met the ambassador the other night," said Hali. "But you never listen, do you?" The dog set the tray beside her. "Gio will be joining us, Colpi. Another cup." He sighed and hobbled back to the pantry. "And some of that leftover pie." She chuckled, then explained for the cat's sake. "My Gio and his sweet tooth."

"I must also apologize for leaving your most informative tour." Scratch followed Gio to the table. "I realized too late that I had misjudged the time. My appointment with Grand Hali was at 0930."

"Technically," said Hali, "I am not a grand." She reached for the cruet of melted butter. "Since I wasn't cloned from one of the Twenty-Two Houses." She poured a dollop into her cup.

"I confess that I'm still learning your ways," Scratch said. "But surely you are grand by marriage to House Barbaro?"

"Sometimes I feel more married to the villa than to these husbands of mine." When she stirred the khave, her spoon clinked against the rim.

Colpi returned with Gio's cup and the remains of the coppernut pie.

"Thank you, Colpi." She patted him on the back. "If you'd leave us now, we'd like some privacy. No interruptions, so please take your good self over to Fra's apartment and leave Gio's wing to us until lunch."

Gio watched Hali pour his kahve with dismay. How to untangle all the secrets twisting in the air above this polite chatter? Clearing his wing of the villa? Hali meeting with an ambassador—if that's what Scratch really was—without Fra? Did Hali know about the cat's connection to the circus? Clearly Scratch was working another scheme. Or was it all part of the same scheme?

"I thought Cranal was the Nearspace ambassador," Gio said. "He's been here less than a year. Not recalled already?"

"Not at all," said Scratch. "My colleague continues to work to normalize relations between our worlds and Boon. He is the political officer. My role is to foster understanding between species here and throughout the Sphere, particularly in the wake of the Cragon fiasco."

"Ancient history." Hali spooned syrup into Gio's cup and passed it to him. "Not an issue anymore. Everyone involved has been dead for almost a century and a half."

"History here perhaps," said Scratch, "but we at Nearspace have long memories. It's how we remain true to ourselves against the staggering immensities of the upside. So, in the interests of full disclosure, Cragon fell apart as a collective enterprise soon after your illustrious founder Pao expelled it from Boon. But many of its worlds and commercial associations have since recombined into a new polity."

"A new polity?" said Gio. "As in the Nearspace Cooperative Sphere?"

"There is a First World saying." Scratch yawned. "About selling old wine in new bottles."

Gio shot Hali a questioning glance and she returned a sardonic smile. Not news to her. "Does Fra know?" he asked.

KING OF THE DOGS, QUEEN OF THE CATS

"I hope not," said Hali.

"And will you tell him?"

Hali helped herself to a slice of the pie before replying. "Will you?" She passed the plate to Scratch. "He'll find out soon enough."

"We trust your judgement," said Scratch. "Nearspace makes no apologies but we understand the need to proceed with consideration. So we begin by disclosing our history to those we believe are most progressive and discreet."

"What do you want from us, Scratch?"

The cat started to take her hat off but Gio snatched it from her. She'd pushed him past annoyance to anger. He peered into it. Nothing. He looked up to see Scratch's fur puffed in alarm and her claws out. Her alarm pleased him. Let her feel threatened for a change.

"Why are you here?" he said.

Her pupils dilated, the cat turned to Hali. Scratch forced a nod that was so stiff Gio thought it might crack her neck. Maybe ambassadors were more touchy than ringmasters.

Hali sighed. "I'm leaving this house," she said. "You and Fra. Boon, as soon as I can."

Gio couldn't help but laugh. It started as a rumbling in his stomach, then a tightness in his throat and then he had to emit some kind of sound or he would explode.

Of course, Hali was leaving. Hilarious. Fra would be disgraced since divorce was for common citizens, not grands. And since so many had questioned Fra's judgment in marrying Hali in the first place, the Barbaros political future would be over. A relief for Gio, except that life in the Villa Barbaro with his embittered senior would now be torture. He laughed because they were giving him the best reason yet to leave home. And then, like the sunlight burning fog away, he understood.

"You knew about circuses." So much now made ominous sense. "You arranged to meet with this cat and now you want to leave. And that means… Did you steer her to me? Help her get me to the New Forest?"

"I knew you be interested in the Ambassador's show." Hali spoke as if inventing new words. "It's where you belong, Gio."

"And growing up." Gio was talking faster, as new revelations came. "Always telling me about the upside. Encouraging me to build my collection."

"There's so much more to the universe than this little planet."

"And Fra?"

"Fra is deluded. He tries to be your famous grand, but he's nothing but Pao Barbaro's ghost."

KING OF THE DOGS, QUEEN OF THE CATS

This was more or less what Gio had come to believe, but hearing Hali put it so bluntly made him cringe. Fra and Hali had been together just a dozen years, but Fra had been Gio's parent, brother, and teacher all his life. As difficult as their relationship had become, he'd helped make Gio the man he was. Once upon a time, Gio had shared his senior's pride in Pao, and his vision of their future greatness.

"Since when was this your plan?"

"There was no plan." Hali hesitated. "When I came to your world, I didn't have many choices. I met Fra. He was good to me. You, on the other hand…" She reached to pat his hand but he jerked it away. "…you were a challenge. You had no use for me, but I'd like to think I won you over. And then we were happy for a while. Content, at least. But after Pry Ullo had his stroke, your senior began to think that maybe the time had come for the Barbaros' return to power. He became so obsessed—but you know all that. He changed. We all changed. I've been miserable for the last year, so when Ambassador Scratak asked a favor in return for passage off Boon, I said yes. You would've too, Gio. To go anywhere I want in the upside? I know you would take that offer."

Gio moaned. He felt like sliding down his chair and hiding under the table.

Scratch patted Gio's hand. "The upside is the future." She took her hat from him. "The Supremacy is Boon's past."

Gio remembered something that Kly had said when she had come to him here at the Villa. Was that just last night? She claimed that she'd defaced the statue of her grand to escape history.

"But why all this maneuvering and secrecy? Revenge on the Barbaros for Cragon's Landing? Are you trying to reconquer the Supremacy?"

"We don't conquer, we cooperate. It's less painful." Scratch put the hat on. "And we'll cooperate with anyone who welcomes change."

"You feel betrayed." Hali leaned toward him and tried to get him to look at her. "But I'm betraying Fra, not you. Because you see things as they really are. You resent being a Barbaro clone, but just think about the differences between you and Fra. He looks at the differences between humans and the uplifted and sees nothing but inferiority. He thinks they deserve to be his servants. You have friends who are dogs. Dogs like you, they trust you. And Fra wants to make Villa Barbaro the Supreme House when the Supremacy is doomed because it depends on a cloning technology that it no longer has."

KING OF THE DOGS, QUEEN OF THE CATS

Gio kept his eyes on the scarred tabletop as he listened, as if he might discover his future in the dark knots and grain of the wood. Hali knew him too well.

"Change is coming." Now it was Scratch's turn. "Den Ullo has had second thoughts about our opening and has called on all humans to stay away."

"Den? What about Pry Ullo?"

"Another stroke, we think. Dying, may already be dead. But whoever is in charge is panicking and with good reason. The Supremacy can't survive a transition of power, once cats and dogs demand their rights. That's inevitable and not our doing. But we're taking steps to prevent your grand houses from stumbling into another bloodbath as they fight over succession. Boon could be sliding toward another Cragon's Landing. We think there's another way."

"And Kly?" said Gio. "Part of your scheme? Has she always been your agent? Or are you controlling her like you're trying to control me?"

"Kly Gamane makes her own decisions," said the cat. "As do you."

"Nobody is controlling you, my dear Gio." Hali rose from the table. "But this is how you can prove it. I'm leaving because I need to." As she passed behind him, her fingertips brushed across his shoulder and he shivered. "So do you. You can't stay here anymore if you're ever going to be Gio and not just the latest Barbaro clone. It's time to leave Fra and this sad mausoleum."

Gio watched them go. He felt the weight of his life to that moment and it seemed to pin him to the hard chair. So he sat staring at half of a coppernut pie and a cup of khave that had gone cold. He had no good choices. He couldn't live with Fra but he didn't trust Scratch. Did he trust Kly? He was surprised to discover he did, but that was because she was at least as naïve as he was. The agents of the Nearspace Cooperative Sphere would know exactly how to manipulate a couple of young and gullible politicians from a backward planet like Boon. Maybe he should leave the Enlightened City, disappear over the mountains and find work on some farm or in one of the towns on the coast. But that was just running away.

Scratch had schemed to present him with an obvious choice, but this was the hardest decision Gio had ever had to make.

ANNOUNCING

Gio knocked a third time. "Fra?" he called.

At first, when he'd tried the door from the Olympus Salon to his senior's wing and found it locked, he'd hoped that nobody would answer. In the moment he would much rather have avoided the storm of emotions that awaited him on the other side of that door. But he knocked again, waited, and then again, each time harder. Despite his dread, he needed to get this last confrontation over with. He'd started for the New Forest and the circus but had turned back when he realized that this was something he ought to do. After all, he'd lived with his senior his entire life. Fra had brought him up, for better or worse, and he wasn't going to leave the Villa Barbaro without saying goodbye.

Knock-knock-*knock*.

Finally he heard a shuffling sound. Gio rolled his head hard left and then right against the tension in his neck. The deadbolt clicked open. The door swung away.

Colpi stood on all fours, gazing up at him in confusion. "The door is locked," he said.

"I know that." Gio hadn't stopped to think of what the servants would make of all this. "I need to talk to Fra."

"He locked the door. When it is talking time, he will unlock it." The old dog's hind legs shifted to one side and he swung wearily away. The door began to close.

"Wait." Gio caught it. "I'm leaving."

Colpi paused to consider this. "Like Hali?"

"No," he said, then realized that poor Colpi might misunderstand; he was not the smartest dog in the Enlightened City. "A little like her, yes."

"I miss her," said Colpi. "She is kind to me. Like you."

"Will he see me?"

"I do not know what is happening, Senator Gio. Why are they hurting us?"

"Senator, Colpi? You're calling me Senator now? I'm your Gio."

"He said to." Colpi licked his lips with his long tongue. "He said to remind you."

KING OF THE DOGS, QUEEN OF THE CATS

Gio took a big gulp of air; this was going to be harder than he'd thought. "Who's hurting you?"

"Enemies."

"You don't have any enemies, Colpi." He scratched between the dog's ears to reassure him. "So how is he? Not good, I'm guessing."

"He smells muddy, Senator Gio." The dog gave a low growl. "Like something was buried." He stood aside and let Gio pass.

The door from Olympus opened onto Fra's library. Gio was shocked by what he saw. It was no surprise that the shelves had been stripped of at least half of his collection. But the floor was strewn with books, some in haphazard piles, others flung open-faced against the wall. He bent to scoop up a couple, straightening the crumpled pages. *The Season of the Smalls. No Red, Blue Love.* He recognized them as Hali's.

Colpi stepped over the mess. "He wants them not moved."

Gio let the books slide back onto the floor and followed.

They passed into the game room where Fra and Gio used to play Molly-Go. They were both fierce competitors; sometimes their kill shots would leave bruises. When Gio was a teenager they were so well matched that they'd had to scrap the win-by-two rule because the games seemed endless. They would encourage each other, compliment pretty returns. Once Fra had said, "Can't outplay me, kid, but you're definitely outworking me." Gio had written that down and posted it on the wall above his desk in his study. Their play had ended when Gio took up lawnball in a serious way and Fra's left elbow developed twinges. Since then Fra had been using the game room for workouts with his weight set and body press, but the Molly table was still leaning against the wall and their pickets hung on the rack.

Colpi hurried ahead of Gio through Hali's dressing room, which Fra had carved out of the master bedroom. It was empty: open drawers and lonely hangers. She'd escaped with her clothes, if not her books.

The dog reached the study before Gio. "Senator Gio is leaving," he blurted, "but not like Hali."

Gio winced at Colpi's childlike gaffe as he stepped through the doorway. He couldn't remember the last time he'd penetrated this far, into Fra's rooms and it took a moment to realize what was different about his senior's study. Normally Fra kept the curtains shut because he was worried about snoops, although Gio had no idea why anyone would care about their doings. Now the curtains were pulled away and afternoon sun filled the room. Fra stood in front of one of the tall windows, his back to his visitors.

"We'll have dinner at the usual time, Colpi." He sounded calm enough, not at all like someone who would assault innocent books. He did not turn around.

Colpi waited, circled once as if unsure whether he'd been dismissed and then padded from the room, closing the door behind him

Fra stayed where he was, staring out at Capital Ward. Pao had built his villa on the height of land in what had since become the enclave of the Twenty-Two Grand Houses. Even though the Barbaro fortunes had declined, they still had the best view in the Enlightened City.

An awkward minute passed as neither Barbaro spoke. Then another crawled by. Gio knew this tactic all too well. Fra liked to use silence to intimidate Gio into confessing, even when he'd done nothing wrong. Gio wasn't about to start this conversation. If he did, he'd be talking to his senior's back. Advantage: Fra. Instead he walked behind the desk and sat in the chair that Hali had teasingly called Fra's throne. It was actually a folding curule seat, too modest in Gio's opinion for royalty, despite all the carving and marquetry. Four S shaped legs supported two broad leather straps, one for the seat, one for the backrest. The feet were sculpted dog's heads and the arms were inlaid with coppernut, cedar and bone. The restored leather squeaked as it took Gio's weight. He glanced around the room as if he'd nothing better to do. On the near wall, the portrait that Pao had commissioned before his rise to power hung above a display case of obsolete guns and needle splits and flashkills—historic junk made of pocked and corroded metal and brittle plastics recovered from the insurrection. As a child, Gio had wondered why his grands had thought preserving the cheap armaments of ancient times was worth the trouble. That was before he'd started his own collection of upside artifacts. On the opposite wall, memorabilia from Fra's time in the Senate was arrayed atop a polished wooden credenza: plaques, belts of copper and silver and an Order of the Sky hat. Gio was surprised to see his lawnball medal there as well. Hali had asked him for it after the Gogos had won the city championship two years ago, and he'd been happy to give it to her. Fra must have appropriated it.

His senior still refused to acknowledge his presence, so Gio hit upon a way to win the stalemate. He pressed a thumb to the reader on the desktop, unlocking all the drawers. Then he opened the top one—slowly, so that the scrape of the slide and the swish of the bearings was audible. Gio didn't really care what it contained, but Fra wouldn't want his traitor clone going through his desk.

"And so where are you going, Senator?" Fra said, still watching from the window.

Gio gave him nothing.

"When you go?" Fra had to turn to face him. "If you go, that is."

"Ambassador Scratak has asked me to join the Antic Tour of Interspecies Marvels."

Fra snorted in scorn. "She's no Ambassador. That cat is a spy sent by the Cragons. Even you must realize that."

"I'm sure she has her own agenda, as do we all. But Nearspace is not the Cragon Collective. And neither of us is Pao Barbaro. Those battles were decided long ago, Fra."

He gave Gio a sour look. "And after the circus? Or is this your new career?"

"I intend to save enough to book passage off Boon."

His expression turned to stone. "You ungrateful idiot." He strode across the room until he loomed over Gio. "You're in my chair."

Gio felt a tingle at the back of his neck. He couldn't believe that Fra wanted a fight, but he could feel his own blood rising. They were Senators, grands of the

Twenty-Two; they didn't argue with their fists. He forced himself to calm down and raised an open hand to show he intended no threat. Fra gave him the smallest possible nod and Gio eased up and away. They stood on either side of the chair for a moment, glowering at each other. Gio often saw his future self when he looked at his clone. How could he not? Now for the first time he realized that because of things he had done and hoped to do, he was no longer doomed to become this man someday. His future would not be determined by his genes nor circumscribed in this decrepit old building. Fra's anger at Gio's defiance, which once would have been scary, now seemed pathetic. He gestured for Fra to sit and then stepped around the desk.

His senior hesitated before sagging into his chair. "Why, Gio?" He leaned back against the leather rest, twined hands behind his neck, stretched elbows out and gave Gio the saddest look he'd ever seen. "Why are you throwing away centuries of work by our grands? Do you think you can stop being a Barbaro?"

"I hope so. I intend to try."

He shook his head. "I'm fifty-two years old." His voice was low, and he might have been musing to himself. "And now I'm supposed to thaw another embryo, spend another twenty years to raise a new junior clone?" He leaned forward and slapped the desktop as if to wake himself up. "But I will." He scowled at Gio. "Don't think I can't replace you."

"I know you can. But then there will be just the one Barbaro clone left. And the Ullos are down to two, if the rumors are true that Den has already thawed Pry's replacement. The Rools and the Choa will go extinct when their current juniors die. The clock is running down on the Supremacy. You need the upsiders to restart the cell transfer lab to create new clones. And the bots that tend your existing embryos in the creche are two centuries old. Nobody on Boon understands these things."

"We still have decades to negotiate new technology transfers. And it has to be on our terms."

"Human terms, you mean. But what about the cats and dogs?"

"Oh right." He always sneered when Gio mentioned animal rights. "When has a cat ever shared anything voluntarily with a dog? Maybe you think we should appoint your lawnball team to the Senate? And if you're so set on equality, let's send Colpi to Nearspace as our trade representative. The only way for the species to get along is equivalence, not equality."

"I don't have all the answers," said Gio. "But I do know things are going to change."

Gio expected him to press the argument, but his heart wasn't in it. "This is her fault." Fra said.

"Hali?"

"Did you know?"

Know what? Gio considered. Even though he had lived with her since he was eleven, he realized now he had no idea who she really was. "I knew she was unhappy. Just like I was. Maybe you were too. You acted like you were."

"I could've done better." Fra was musing again. "I see that now. I'm sorry."

It didn't feel to Gio as if the murmured apology was intended for him. For who then? Hali? The dead Barbaros?

Fra absently reached across the desk for the glass jar filled with sweetbuttons. Their favorite. Gio had the identical jar on his desk in the Senate. Fra lifted the lid and retrieved a handful of the multicolored candies. Then he seemed to remember that Gio was watching him. "Want some?" He shook the jar.

"No thank you."

His senior considered, then nodded. "You should go," he said. "My door is locked because I need to think. Colpi should never have let you in." He made a sweeping gesture across his desk. "Go play with your circus friends." He gave a bitter laugh. "I'd advise you not to trust the cat, but you're not taking advice anymore."

Gio thought he should say something else, but he wasn't sure what. He opened the study door, then turned for a last look. "Goodbye, Fra."

Fra was staring at the portrait of Pao Barbaro. "He's watching." He pointed at it, then shook his finger at their grand. "He never stops watching."

INTERSPECIES

Troq was one of the more quarrelsome cats Gio had ever met. While he'd always favored dogs, not least because of his Barbaro heritage, he got along fine with cats. Most cats. So why did this one irk him so often? And why did Scratch have to put them together in the same act?

Troq was in line at the meatserve ahead of him. "It's the hands," said the cat. She was chatting with Kly, who was already at the meatserve filling her bowl. "Humans think it's creepy that we walk on our hands."

"Doesn't bother me." Kly brushed the lip of her bowl against the edge of the dispenser to dislodge the last blob of cultured ground meat. "That's what walking gloves are for." She stepped aside to wait for Gio.

Troq set her bowl under the dispenser. "Yes, but then we go barehanded sometimes." She flipped the mix switch from *ground* to *slurry* and a viscous ruby stream oozed into her bowl. "You're disgusted, but it's not like you don't go barefooted."

"Except we don't put our feet in our mouths," said Gio.

"You do plenty of unsanitary things with your hands."

"Like what?"

"Would you two stop," said Kly, "before I lose my appetite?"

"See you in there." Troq purred as she headed for the dining room.

Gio switched the meatserve back to *ground*.

All of the cats and many of the dogs in the show ate their rations raw, but Kly and Gio preferred cooked meals, even though the upsiders' synthmeat was sterilized. As usual, they had no problem finding free burners on the stove. Gio set Kly to dicing onions while he poured the ground meat into a frying pan next to the pot of noodle sauce. Although most food in the dorm tent was printed, Scratch had arranged for selected fresh produce to be delivered for the only two humans in her show.

"Smells good," said Kly. "Ready for me?"

KING OF THE DOGS, QUEEN OF THE CATS

Gio eyed the uneven mess she had made of the onion: some flat bits were the size of his thumb, other skinny slices were centimeters long. Kitchen skills had not been part of Kly's education. He gave her an approving smile. "Sure, dump them in."

Gio felt lucky to have Kly helping him adjust to circus life. They'd been inseparable since he'd come to the New Forest. Every day they trained together, cooked together, ate together, rehearsed together and slept together. Gio had wanted to be an acrobat, but his athletic skills were limited to sprinting across lawns, jumping fences and winging balls through hoops. So Scratch had cast him in Kly's clown act, impressing on him that it was important for the show's higher purpose that the humans shed their privilege—and their dignity.

Troq was more than content to help with this.

When they sat at the clown table, Liffy and Troq were discussing taxonomy. "Cats are obligate carnivores," Troq said, "and dogs are scavenging carnivores."

"We're not scavengers," said Liffy, "not since we uplifted. So what if I eat some veggies? Sweetmelon? An occasional slice of pie? I'm an opportunist when it comes to food." He finished licking his bowl clean and turned it over so that the cleaning bots would take it away. "Besides, you eat bugs."

"Once in a while and only to honor them for their entertainment value." Troq was a talker; she was so busy dominating conversation that it took her twice as long to eat as the other clowns. "If I'm going to spend time chasing them, eating them becomes part of the deal." Her shocking pink tongue flicked into the meat slurry.

The dining room tables were built low to the ground, so that the uplifted could stand on them and eat comfortably, lowering their heads into their bowls. This meant that Gio and Kly had to sit on the concrete of the launch pad and scoot their legs under the table so that everyone would be on the same level.

"I thought dogs were omnivores." Gio slurped noodles. "Like us."

"No," said Kly. "I read that on the First World, Liffy's ancestors ate nothing but meat."

"Dead meat," said Troq. "The way scavengers like it."

Liffy bared his teeth behind a good-natured growl and the cat batted at the air in response. Gio was a little jealous at how well the two of them got along.

"Good evening, everyone." Scratch turned one of the jugglers' barrels on end then hopped up to address the performers. "Just two days to the opening and we're on schedule. I've just come from the Big Top on the West

KING OF THE DOGS, QUEEN OF THE CATS

Lawn. The bots will finish printing the stands tonight. Which means we're ready for dress tomorrow. Remember this is a closed rehearsal. Friends and families can come to a performance after opening night."

"They can't get tickets," someone shouted.

"We're setting aside a block for 2/11." Scratch said. "Heavily discounted."

Grumbles and moans. "That's not until next week," another voice cried.

"I call that good news, since the first six shows are sold out. Remember, what we hope to accomplish won't happen opening night. Or opening week. We're in this for the long term."

She paused for the applause and yips and meows of approval to fade.

"Thanks to all of you who helped paper the city with ads. We won't be releasing any more tickets until we see how the Supremacy reacts."

Troq's voice dropped. "There'll be riots if the Ullos try to shut us down."

"Which is why they won't dare," Liffy's nostrils flared.

Gio and Kly exchanged worried glances.

"No, really," said Liffy. "My brother Riff is police and he says most of them won't obey orders to close us."

The tip of his tongue stretched and curled. "You met him, Gio. The one who first sent you out here."

"Let's have updates from the acts." Scratch produced a handheld from her doublet. "From the top and no comments from the cheap seats." She checked the screen. "Spectacle?"

Performers from all fourteen acts were to make a grand entry at the opening of the show. The tumblers would lead the parade and the tumbler captain called out, "Marching order is all set."

"Good," said Scratch. "Remember to keep things moving no matter who you spot in the audience. And save the styling for your blow offs. Next is Jic and Boc and Their Impossible Walking Ladders."

Boc said, "We fixed the trick with the extensions." She was a tall woman and Jic was a short man; switching their mismatched ladders had been trouble all week.

"Music cues?"

"Done."

"Good." Scratch scanned the dining area for the next act. "Forty-Four Footfall Follies?"

The hand and foot jugglers complained about the bots picking up their props, especially the knives and plates.

KING OF THE DOGS, QUEEN OF THE CATS

Scratch made a note of this. "Trapeze? Named your act yet?"

Awkward silence. Then a skinny poodle spoke up. "We can't agree on one."

"Because you want top billing," a cat cried and two others stood in silent support, tails switching.

"By tomorrow." Scratch pointed at the unhappy troupe. "Or I'll name you myself. Zany Slingshot Cats?"

"We've got our dismount set."

It took another few minutes for Scratch to get through the list. "Clowns?" she said finally. "What are we calling your skit?"

Liffy had proposed a compromise that none of them liked. "Dinnertime Madness?" Everyone could hear the uncertainty in his voice.

"Blah." Scratch pulled her hat off in disgust. "You're the show closer and you're featuring our only grands. Sharper, people. Sharper. We want everybody talking about you."

As the meeting broke up, the four of them agreed to gather in Gio and Kly's room in an hour. Gio fetched beer for Kly and Liffy; Troq preferred her own intoxicant.

"Why do we even need a name?" Kly curled on the bed next to Liffy. "Our skit is tight. It's funny."

"And edgy." Gio sat on the floor, back against the wall.

"And messy." Troq shook catnip from an envelope into her hand.

Grunts of approval all around. The running joke was that it was harder to clean the sticky residue from the skit off themselves than it was to remove their clown makeup.

"We should name it after you two." Troq pressed catnip to her nose leather with one hand and caught what fell away with the other. She sniffed that as well.

"Something Grand?" Kly poured another beer into Liffy's bowl.

Troq sneezed and blew fluff across the room.

"Something Grand Something." Gio balanced a third beer box on his stack. "Something."

Troq rolled onto her back. "The Only Grands Dumb Enough to Join the Circus." Her legs pumped air as if to punctuate each word.

"Brave enough." Liffy.

Gio laughed. "Dumb enough works for me." Now he was agreeing with Troq?

"I mean, why is our skit funny?" said Kly. "Maybe that's the clue."

"Because it's surprising." Gio remembered what she'd said that first day. "Improper without giving offense."

KING OF THE DOGS, QUEEN OF THE CATS

"By the way, you all don't have to hold back." Kly patted the side of Liffy's neck. "You're not going to hurt me."

"Are you four working or playing?" Scratch stuck her head in the door. "Dress rehearsal tomorrow."

"Both," said Kly. "Why are we funny?"

"You're funny...?" Scratch considered. "Depends on the audience. For the uplifted, individually not funny. But they'll worry about what's going to happen when they see you all together. Interspecies mayhem is scary to them. Then things do go wrong, but not wrong in the way they imagined."

"So they laugh." Kly nodded. "Because they're relieved."

Gio said, "But the humans in the audience will see something different."

"Right," said Liffy. "They'll laugh at dogs and cats pretending to be intelligent. Like we're real people. Because to them that either makes us look ridiculous—or cute."

"Cute is worse," Troq said.

Liffy's ears were drooping. "Like we have no clue who we really are. Because humans know that dogs aren't as smart as them. Or even as smart as cats."

Troq hissed. "You're smarter than most humans."

"Oh thanks." Liffy said sardonically. He sat on his hind legs and waved his forelegs in the air like a puppy waiting for a treat. "That's sort of like a human saying I'm above average for a dog."

"Stop it, you two," said Scratch. "The humans who argue that averages limit your development are the stupidest humans there are. Your job is to make them smarter."

After a glum silence, Troq staggered to her feet. "No offense meant to all the smart dogs in dog-dom." She made her uncertain way across the room to Liffy and, for some reason, licked him on his floppy ear.

"None taken." Liffy's eyes went wide, but he stood still for a second and a third lick.

"What if no humans come?" Now Kly sounded depressed. "I mean, there's just a handful of us in the show and now Den Ullo calls for a boycott and why would they pay to see their servants juggle and besides, the grands will turn everybody against us because we're embarrassing them."

"They'll come," said Scratch. "I have a plan. But stop trying to talk yourselves out of a good time. This show is already a hit." She flicked a finger against her hat, making a soft *plonk*. "Get some sleep. Clowning is hard work."

But Kly couldn't sleep. Long after everyone had left and the lights were out she rolled over to Gio. "Hold me?"

KING OF THE DOGS, QUEEN OF THE CATS

Drowsy and obedient, he draped an arm over her.

"I'm worried," she whispered. "I wasn't before, but I am now."

"Opening night nerves. You heard the cat: this show is a hit." He nibbled at her ear. "I could try to cure your jitters for you." He ran a hand down her thigh.

He expected that she would either swing a leg on top of him or else put him off with a caress, but instead she was ominously silent.

"Okay, worried." He yawned and shook himself awake. "Worried about what?"

"Everything."

"What, like the tent falling down? A meteor strike?"

She gave him an nudge. "Aren't you worried?"

He wasn't. He hadn't thought much about the future after he'd left the Villa Barbaro; he was too busy learning his part. And being with Kly. "It's a good show and if people don't like one act, there's a better one right behind."

"Except us."

"Have you been paying attention at rehearsal, Kly? Scratch deliberately saved the best for last."

"But it has to be more than a show. Did you leave the Villa Barbaro for 'just a show?'"

Actually, he had. But he propped himself on an elbow and stared at the shadow that he knew must be her face. "Why did you leave Gamane House?"

She'd told him how she didn't get along with Chu, mostly because of her drinking. But Chu spent most of her time at her country estate, paid no attention to her senatorial duties and had let Kly do pretty much whatever she wanted. She was so uninterested in the Supremacy that she probably wouldn't have cared if Kly told her about blowing the face off the statue of Leeol Gamane.

"Nobody was paying attention to me," she said. "I did what senators were supposed to do, I went to meetings, I did the research and I made speeches. Everybody knows we're stuck and that the Ullos have no idea how to get us unstuck. We need to get the species working together before we can change things."

"I know that." He reached in the darkness and found her cheek with his fingertips. "And that's what we're doing here. And having fun besides. So what's to worry about?"

"I don't know. That it won't do any good. Or maybe if we make changes, they'll be the ones that Scratch wants."

"Now you're sounding like Fra."

Silence.

KING OF THE DOGS, QUEEN OF THE CATS

"Okay, we know she's using us. She's using all the performers, but you and me, especially. I mean, people look at me and they're going to see Pao Barbaro. Maybe I'm supposed to be some kind of symbol. But whatever else she wants, she also wants what we want. Which means that if she's using us, we're using her to get what we want."

"You said 'want' too many times. Maybe when we get back to the Senate, you should hire a speechwriter."

"Oh, are we going back to the Senate?"

"Someday. When they have to listen to us."

They were still so new together that Gio hadn't told her that he hoped to leave Boon and tour the upside. He decided this wasn't the time to bring it up. "Okay then." He leaned toward her in the darkness. "Maybe I'll get you to write my speeches." His kiss landed not on her lips but on the side of her nose. She squawked and used her hand to guide him to the proper alignment.

They were getting good at kissing. It came with practice.

"I know that Scratch has a plan," she said finally. "I'm just not sure that it's the right one for us. That's why I came to your room that night. I needed someone to talk to about all this."

"You did more than talk."

"I remember." The whisper of her breath on his chest hair tickled. "I think that part worked out all right."

"More than all right." He pressed against her. "And the talking part?"

She didn't immediately reply. He was so close to her that he could feel her swallow.

"What's our plan, Gio?" she said.

"We do the show…"

"That's hers. Do *we* have one?" She shushed him. "A plan that isn't about the show?"

The strangest thing happened then. Even though it was dark, too dark to make out the woman next to him, Gio felt his life light up with the realization that he was having an *adventure*. Not only that, but he thought he could see the two of them shining with all the adventures they might someday have together. Yes, he had questions and, of course, the tomorrow was a mystery, but Gio had never had an adventure until now. It had been Kly who'd brought him to this bed in this tent in this amazing circus. His blood pounded and his skin felt tight and his mind seemed to stretch toward a future that had no set shape but that dazzled with possibility. To get there he would have to become himself, Gio Barbaro, but he would need her to do that. They would have adventures together. This one and the next one and the one after that.

And then the moment passed. How long had it lasted? Seconds? Minutes? A lifetime? All he knew for sure was that Kly was waiting for his answer. He was ready now. He knew exactly what to say.

"Yes we have a plan," he said. "You and I are the plan."

CIRCUS

The air inside the Big Top felt heavy and wet, so maybe it was the heat generated by thirteen hundred cats, dogs and humans that was making Gio sweat. All that shouting, clapping, stomping, barking, caterwauling and laughing was giving The Antic Tour of Interspecies Marvels its own weather. Or maybe Gio's nerves were the reason that his clown costume was soaked. As he rehearsed gags in his head, he was developing his own case of opening night jitters. Yet what scared him most was the realization that when he stepped into the ring for his act there would be no going back to the Villa Barbaro or Fra. Yes, he had left that life already, but that had been a private leaving. This was a public announcement of who he now was. When had he ever done anything so final?

"…so many of them." Kly leaned close to make herself heard over the audience. The artists' lounge was under the stands. "This is working! So happy."

"Yes." He squeezed her hand. "Turnaway sellout. Good."

She shook her head because he didn't understand. "Humans!" She cupped a hand around his ear and yelled. "So many humans."

Gio had seen them during the grand entry of all the acts. Despite Den Ullo's desperate call for a boycott, almost a quarter of the audience was human. The freighter *Faraway* had arrived on Boon three weeks before and its crew had been sampling the pleasures of the Enlightened City. Scratch had invited them to the opening and they in turn had brought along the new acquaintances they'd made. Easy to get a date when you were a rich spacer from the upside.

"And now, citizens of Boon and friends from the stars, please turn your attention to the two masts which hold our tent upright." Scratch's amplified voice was muffled by the crush of bodies above them. "Notice the wire stretched between them. What's that, you can't? Too far away, you say? The reason the wire is so hard to see is that it is just six centimeters wide."

The band played a flourish.

"*And* it's suspended some twelve meters above the center ring."

Another flourish.

"And now, as we rig a safety net to protect our daring funambulists, please welcome the Cat Dancers and their Dog Jumparoos."

When the audience stamped approval, it was like an attack. Kly's head tilted up at the avalanche of sound, her eyes bright with excitement. Gio was pleased that he'd been able to help her past her midnight doubts, but he didn't want her to see how uneasy he now was. Liffy was spooked too. He lay flat, paws tight against his muzzle. A crown that read "King of the Dogs" was glued to the top of his head, slightly off center. He was draped in a purple robe that was way too long so he could sell all the tripping gags in the script. Gio crouched to give his friend a reassuring pat, remembering how he had found Liffy shivering at the Founders' Day fireworks two years ago.

The applause abated and Scratch began narrating the wire walk.

"Rise, Your Majesty," said Gio. "You look like a rug down there."

Liffy snorted and got up. "Don't forget who's boss, Boss," he said, hind leg scratching furiously at his neck.

The artists' lounge was nothing but a rectangle of tilt-up partitions and a scatter of chairs. The production crew had set out bowls of flavored water and bland crunchy snacks that nobody was touching. Gio stood and stretched, wishing he could slip out to the lawn to run some laps. There was nothing to do but wait. And listen. The audience loved the show so far. But that didn't mean they'd love the clowns. Especially the human clowns.

Troq yawned. Her crown, labelled "Queen of the Cats," rode forward on her head and her red robe was ridiculously short, more bib than garment. She looked more uncomfortable than nervous; several times he had seen her turn to groom herself with her tongue, only to realize that her fur was slathered in pink makeup.

"Prepare yourselves," Scratch's voice rumbled, "for Zook Skywalker and the Hoops of Doom."

At the dress rehearsal the night before, they had voted Kly to be their captain. She nodded to them now. They were next. Time to move from the lounge to backstage.

KING OF THE DOGS, QUEEN OF THE CATS

"Ahh…" Gio's gut twisted and his tongue felt as big as a lawnball. "Be right ba…" He plunged away, staggering blind beneath the stands until he butted against the fabric wall of the tent. When he vomited, he tried to foul the smallest possible spot. Make it easy for someone to clean up after him. Someone? He wiped the corner of his eye. Not some poor caretaker dog, he hoped. A bot. Scratch had so many bots. His spit tasted bitter. Maybe that's all Boon really needed. He felt stronger now that his stomach had emptied. Maybe that was the cat's plan. The upsiders would give them bots and bots make everything right.

He was making his way to backstage when the message came.

Messaging 2/04/498 Time 2122

Fra: Listen, Gio, please listen to this. Our moment has arrived. Pry Ullo has been dead thirteen days and Den was keeping it secret. Nobody knew. Nobody. Den has fled the Enlightened City and the grands are gathering at the Senate. We are the flesh and blood of Pao Barbaro, you and I. There is greatness in us. I get why you were unhappy and I approve of your relationship with that spy. We can use your connection to help our cause. With

Nearspace as ally, no other house can challenge us.

History is about to be made and we can make it.

Do you understand? Reply.

Fra: I need you to reply, Gio. Please.

Fra: Reply.

End Session 2/04/498 Time 2123

Gio understood better than Fra ever would. Nobody knew Pry Ullo was dead? He snorted. That was a joke. Scratch had known, she had to. There was a collective shout from the audience. The music swelled and he heard Scratch bellow. "Three flaming hoops, citizens. *Three!*" He couldn't remember the last time Fra had said please to him.

Didn't matter now.

Kly gave him a questioning look as he arrived backstage. He grinned. "No worries," he said, then bent so she could slip the golden leash over his head. The band played their intro and he picked up the flimsy table and collapsing chair and handed his lead to Troq.

"Free citizens of the world," shouted Scratch, "here now are the King of the Dogs and the Queen of the Cats."

The four clowns burst into the blaze and boom of the ring.

KING OF THE DOGS, QUEEN OF THE CATS

In the skit, Liffy and Troq were royalty, Gio and Kly their woebegone servants. After placing the tables and chairs, the four paraded around the ring with Gio trotting on his leash like an obedient pet by Queen Troq's side while King Liffy tugged the willful Kly behind him. A moment of stunned silence was followed by a buzz as the two senators were recognized then the audience bellowed with laughter. At least, the dogs and cats did. If any humans booed, nobody heard them.

The clowns mimed while Scratch narrated. The King and Queen were hungry and their bumbling servants must feed them. But the royals were inept as well. Liffy kept tripping over his robe, to be saved by Kly in a variety of awkward and suggestive poses. And when Gio tried to seat Troq, the chair or table or both would collapse. After finally settling their masters, the humans fetched heaping platters of noodles topped with a slime green sauce. There followed an intricate choreography of near disaster as they tried to pass one another, bump away, rebalance dangerously tilting platters and try again.

"Careful, careful!" cried Scratch. "Watch where you're going, you clumsy animals."

Finally came a collision that neither human could recover from. They stumbled to opposite sides of the ring, scattering heaps of noodles along the way and dropped their burdens. As the Queen stormed over to rebuke Gio, she took a spectacular pratfall on a sauce slick. Meanwhile Gio was picking up handfuls of noodles from the ground and piling them back on the platter. Troq bounced up, grabbed noodles from Gio and hit him in the chest with a wad of them. Meanwhile Liffy had formed a noodle wig and set it on Kly's head. When the King and Queen had finished humiliating the humans, they stalked haughtily back to their seats to await the next course.

"And yet these foolish and sad creatures," said Scratch, who hovered beside Kly, "have the nerve to resent their betters. Get up, get up!" she called to the kneeling Gio. "There's still work to do."

The roar from the crowd almost lifted the roof off the tent.

Gio strode angrily to Kly and got into a fierce but silent argument over who was at fault, which only ended when he snatched some of Kly's fallen noodles and hurled them into the stands. Kly darted across the ring to do the same with some of Gio's heap. He threw into the seats again, and dared her copy him again, so she did. The audience was screaming with laughter, even those ducking the onslaught.

KING OF THE DOGS, QUEEN OF THE CATS

Then, without warning, a lump of noodles flew back out of the stands. It skidded at Gio's feet. For a second, he stared in disbelief. The crowd caught its breath as well. It was one thing for cats and dogs to throw food at a human—a senator!—in a skit for a laugh, but this was—could be—serious. This wasn't in the script.

Time to improvise.

A laugh bubbled out of Gio as he grabbed as much of the returned noodles as he could and flung them back the way they had come. He was waggling his fingers in mock reprimand when more noodles came his way. He returned fire. Across the ring, Kly was also engaged in a vigorous noodle-based defense.

Now the sound was so deafening, it seemed to stop time. Afterward Gio was not sure how long Scratch had let the food fight go on. Seconds? Minutes? A lifetime?

"Your Majesties," Scratch announced finally, "It's time for dessert."

Which, of course, was pie.

UNDERWAY

After the fourth curtain call, Gio began to wonder if the audience would ever leave, although he was gratified that, of all the acts, the clowns were by far the favorite. While Scratch had called the other acts out to take their bows, the clowns were able to change out of their filthy costumes and wipe most of the pie, green sauce and makeup off their faces.

As the last ovation subsided, Scratch raised her arms for an announcement. "Citizens of Boon, dogs, cats and humans, this has been The Antic Tour of Interspecies Marvels, which was brought to you by the Nearspace Cooperative Sphere. For me as your ringmaster, the greatest marvel of this evening has been the way the three species have cooperated to entertain and amaze us all."

This seemed to refresh the crowd's capacity for applause. Scratch spent another thirty seconds waiting for them to settle.

"This cooperation and mutual respect," she continued, "is the way we, in the Nearspace Cooperative, believe free and equal citizens ought to behave. I regret to say there are those on Boon who do not share that belief. Of course you know this, and have no need of an upsider to point it out."

As boisterous as the crowd had been during the performance, it now went silent as a cave.

Gio pulled Kly close. "Pry is dead," he whispered. "And Den is gone. The Ullos are finished."

She goggled at him in astonishment.

"I had a message from Fra." He tapped at his earstone. "This is about to get very political. Always been her plan."

"But after one show?" She shook her head. "It's much too soon."

Scratch filled his voice with portent. "I have just been informed that Pry Ullo…"

"No, *no*." Kly grabbed for his hand. "What is she doing?"

"…and at this very moment, they're gathering in the Senate…"

"Everything will fall apart." She was squeezing his

hand hard enough to crack his knuckles.

At he looked at the anxious cats and dogs and humans in the crowd, Gio realized that he might never get to leave Boon for the upside.

Scratch pointed dramatically toward the capital. "…that we should march there now and present a united front…"

"Gio, what should we do? Whose side are we on here? Gio?"

He was at once thrilled and horrified to feel the spirit of Pao Barbaro stir in him for the first time. But he was Gio and he had Kly to remind him of who he hoped to be. So let the upsiders try to use them; he'd find a way to do what was right.

"We're on our side, Kly," he said. "You and I are the side we're on."

People stared at their two senators as the cat's challenge sank in to the crowd. Nobody had been fooled, not the cats or dogs or humans. The circus had never been just a show. Gio raised Kly's hand for all to see and they started toward Scratch. The cat waited for them, hat off, in the center of the ring.

The other artists parted to let them pass. Everyone realized now who the stars of the show were.